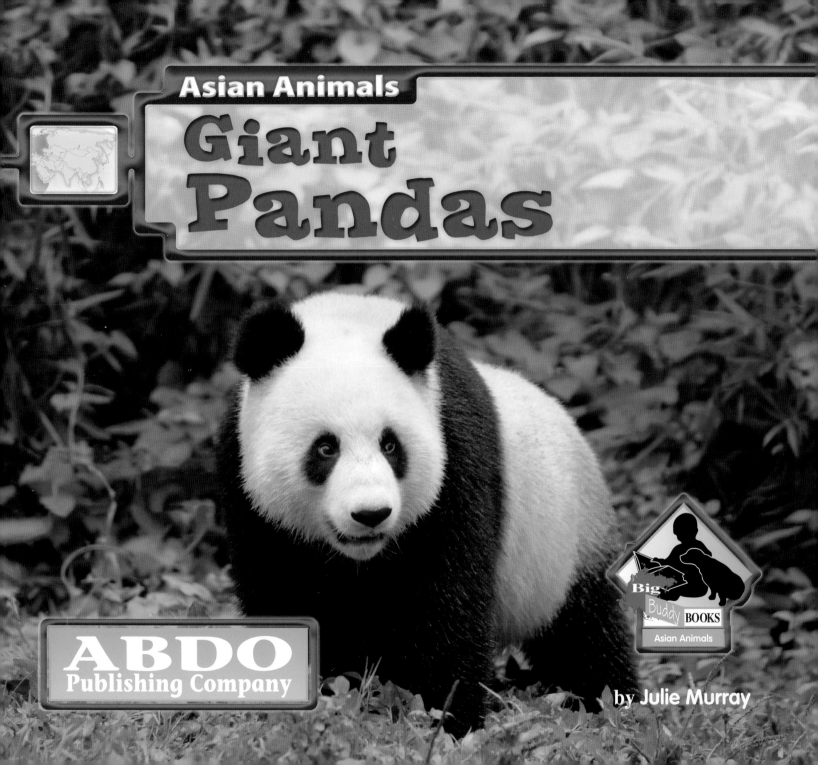

Asian Animals

Giant Pandas

ABDO
Publishing Company

by Julie Murray

Big Buddy BOOKS
Asian Animals

VISIT US AT
www.abdopublishing.com

Printed in the United States of America, North Mankato, Minnesota.
082012
012013

 PRINTED ON RECYCLED PAPER

Coordinating Series Editor: Rochelle Baltzer
Editor: Marcia Zappa
Contributing Editors: Stephanie Hedlund, Sarah Tieck
Graphic Design: Maria Hosley
Cover Photograph: *iStockphoto*: ©iStockphoto.com/ytwong.
Interior Photographs/Illustrations: *Fotosearch.com*: © Corbis (p. 21), © mflippo (p. 27); *Getty Images*: Thomas Kokta/
    Peter Arnold Images (p. 29), Visuals Unlimited, Inc./Robert Pickett (p. 11), Keren Su (p. 15), Wang Xiweil/
    ChinaFotoPress (p. 23), ZSSD/Minden Pictures (p. 17); *Glow Images*: Arco Images GmbH Reinhard, H.
    (p. 7), Arco Images GmbH Strange, K. (p. 9), Dani Carlo/Prisma RM (p. 25), © Daniel J. Cox/CORBIS (p. 5),
    Tom Soucek/Verge Images (p. 13), Superstock (p. 21); *iStockphoto*: ©iStockphoto.com/HU-JUN (p. 4); *Photo
    Researchers, Inc.*: China Press Service (p. 23); *Shutterstock*: Hung Chung Chih (pp. 19, 26), Pichugin Dmitry
    (p. 8), Image Focus (p. 4), Izmael (p. 9), TonyV3112 (p. 8).

Library of Congress Cataloging-in-Publication Data

Murray, Julie, 1969-
  Giant pandas / Julie Murray.
    p. cm. -- (Asian animals)
  ISBN 978-1-61783-553-7
  1. Giant panda--Juvenile literature. I. Title.
  QL737.C27M8899 2013
  599.789--dc23
                        2012023976

Contents

Long ago, nearly all land on Earth was one big mass. About 200 million years ago, the land began to break into **continents**. One of these continents is Asia.

Giant pandas are a type of bear. They are known for their black-and-white fur.

Asia is the largest **continent**. It includes many countries and **cultures**. It also has different types of land and interesting animals. One of these animals is the giant panda. In the wild, giant pandas are only found in Asia.

Giant Panda Territory

Giant pandas are found in small areas of China. China is a country in eastern Asia. Giant pandas live in thick forests high in the mountains. These forests are usually cool, misty, and rainy.

China

6

Another Asian animal called the red panda shares the giant panda's name. But, these animals are not related. The red panda looks like a raccoon with reddish-brown fur.

Giant pandas live in forests mostly filled with bamboo and evergreen trees.

7

Welcome to Asia!

If you took a trip to where giant pandas live, you might find…

…lots of people.

Giant pandas are shy and avoid people. Yet, they live in the country with the world's largest population! China has more than 1.3 billion people. That is about 20 percent of all the people on Earth.

…wild land.

The Tibetan Highlands is in southwestern China. It is high, flat land surrounded by mountains. The Tibetan Highlands is often very dry and cold. Many giant pandas live in the forests on its eastern edge.

...Chinese characters.

Northern Chinese is the official language in China. This language is often called Mandarin in English. Chinese writing uses characters instead of alphabet letters. Each character represents a word or part of a word.

...a rich history.

China has one of the world's oldest societies. Chinese people invented paper and the compass. And, they built amazing structures such as the Great Wall of China (*right*).

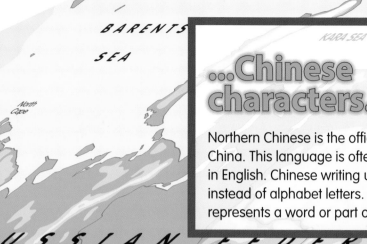

Take a Closer Look

Giant pandas have rounded bodies like other bears. Their tails are small compared to their bodies. A panda's large head has a snout, small round ears, and small eyes.

Giant pandas have thick fur. White fur covers a panda's body and head. A panda has black fur on its legs and across its shoulders. Black fur is also on its ears and around its eyes.

A panda's thick fur keeps it warm high in the mountains, where the air is cool.

Adult giant pandas are large animals. They are two to three feet (0.6 to 0.9 m) tall at their shoulders. They are five to six feet (1.5 to 1.8 m) long. And, they weigh 200 to 300 pounds (90 to 140 kg).

Uncovered!

Male giant pandas are larger than females.

Giant pandas have thick bones. This makes them somewhat heavy for their size.

13

Independent Life

Adult giant pandas generally live alone. They stay in certain home areas. But, their home areas often include shared land.

A giant panda's home area is about two square miles (5 sq km). When food is hard to find, that area may be bigger.

Giant pandas do not have a home that they live in. But, they may sleep in hollow trees or caves. Some small giant pandas sleep high in trees.

Even though giant pandas live alone, they **communicate** with each other. They use their scents to mark their home areas. This lets other pandas know where they are.

Giant pandas sometimes visit each other's home areas. They do this to **mate**. And, giant panda mothers share their home areas with their young.

Uncovered!
Another way giant pandas communicate is by making sounds. These include bleats, growls, and honks.

Giant panda mothers live with their young for up to three years. They communicate often as they teach skills and play.

Mealtime

Giant pandas mainly eat bamboo. They eat bamboo shoots, stems, and leaves from the forests they live in.

It takes a lot of bamboo to fill a giant panda. A panda needs to eat 20 to 85 pounds (9 to 39 kg) of bamboo a day to get enough **nutrients**! So, giant pandas spend at least 12 hours a day eating.

Uncovered!
Giant pandas eat during the day or night. Most of the time they aren't eating is spent sleeping.

Bamboo shoots and leaves have the most nutrients. So, giant pandas eat these first when available.

Giant pandas have special body parts that help them eat bamboo. Their front paws each have an extra-long wristbone covered in skin. Giant pandas use them like thumbs to hold bamboo stems.

Giant pandas have strong **jaws** and cheeks. And, they have large, flat back teeth. These help pandas crush thick, hard bamboo stems.

Giant pandas must drink water every day. Usually, they drink from rivers or streams.

Giant pandas often eat while sitting on their rears.

Baby Pandas

Giant pandas are mammals. Before a female gives birth, she finds a safe place for a den. This could be a hollow tree. A female usually has one or two babies. She gives birth every two to three years.

Baby giant pandas are called cubs. At birth, they weigh only three to five ounces (85 to 142 g). A cub is about the size of a stick of butter! Newborn giant panda cubs are blind and helpless.

Uncovered!
In the wild, giant panda mothers can only raise one baby at a time. So if they have two, they must choose one to raise and leave the other to die.

Giant panda cubs are born with thin, white fur. It changes as they grow.

23

At first, a giant panda mother stays with her newborn cub. The cub drinks its mother's milk and grows. Later, a mother leaves her cub in their den while she finds food and water.

After two to three months, a giant panda cub begins to crawl. At six months to two years, it stops drinking milk. After one and a half to three years, a cub is ready to live on its own.

Giant panda cubs are known for being curious and playful.

Survivors

Life in Asia isn't easy for giant pandas. Long ago, they lived throughout southeast Asia. Now, much of their habitat has been cut down for logging, buildings, and farms. This makes it hard for pandas to find food and mate.

Giant pandas are endangered. This means they are in great danger of dying out.

Scientists believe only 1,000 to 2,000 giant pandas remain on Earth.

Uncovered!

For many people, the giant panda is a symbol for endangered animals. This means it represents all animals in danger of dying out.

Still, giant pandas **survive**. China has set aside forests for them to live in. And, scientists work to help them **mate** in zoos. Someday, they hope pandas born in zoos will be able to live in the wild. Giant pandas help make Asia an amazing place!

In the wild, giant pandas live up to 20 years.

Wow!
I'll bet you never knew...

...that giant pandas are good movers. Giant pandas may seem slow and lazy. But, they can climb trees, swim, and even do somersaults!

...that a common Chinese name for the giant panda means "large bear-cat."

...that giant pandas in zoos around the world belong to China. China loans them to zoos for certain periods of time.

Important Words

communicate (kuh-MYOO-nuh-kayt) to share knowledge, thoughts, or feelings.

continent one of Earth's seven main land areas.

culture (KUHL-chuhr) the arts, beliefs, and ways of life of a group of people.

habitat a place where a living thing is naturally found.

jaws a mouthpart that allows for holding, crushing, and chewing.

mammal a member of a group of living beings. Mammals make milk to feed their babies and usually have hair or fur on their skin.

mate to join as a couple in order to reproduce, or have babies.

nutrient (NOO-tree-uhnt) something found in food that living beings take in to live and grow.

snout a part of the face, including the nose and the mouth, that sticks out. Some animals, such as giant pandas, have a snout.

survive to continue to live or exist.

Web Sites

To learn more about giant pandas, visit ABDO Publishing Company online. Web sites about giant pandas are featured on our Book Links page. These links are routinely monitored and updated to provide the most current information available.

www.abdopublishing.com

Index